Contents

MEET TEAM DENNIS!

If you're reading this **boomic**, you just joined the COOLEST team in the WORLD! Here are some awesome new friends you're about to meet . . .

'Book' + 'comic', geddit?

DENNIS
BEANOTOWN'S PRANKMASTER-GENERAL!

GNASHER
DENNIS'S AWESOME DOG HAS FEARSOME TEETH THAT CAN SMASH CONCRETE!

MINNIE
DENNIS'S COUSIN, WHO KNOWS THAT SHE'S THE REAL LEADER OF THE TEAM!

BEA
DENNIS'S LITTLE SISTER HAS A STONKING BIG PERSONALITY – AND STINKING BIG NAPPIES!

BEANO®

DENNIS & GNASHER
LITTLE MENACE'S GREAT ESCAPE

I. P. DALEY
Craig Graham Mike Stirling

Illustrated by
Nigel Parkinson

First published in Great Britain 2023 by Farshore
An imprint of HarperCollins*Publishers*
1 London Bridge Street, London, SE1 9GF
www.farshore.co.uk

HarperCollins*Publishers*
Macken House, 39/40 Mayor Street Upper,
Dublin 1, D01 C9W8, Ireland

Written by I.P. Daley, Craig Graham & Mike Stirling
Illustrated by Nigel Parkinson
Additional Illustration – Ed Stockham
Senior Creative Services Manager – Usha Chauhan
Executive Producer – Rob Glenny
Text design by Janene Spencer

BEANO.COM

A Beano Studios Product © DC Thomson Ltd (2023)

ISBN 978 0 0085 3404 2
Printed and bound in the UK using 100% renewable electricity at CPI Group (UK) Ltd
001

RUBI VON SCREWTOP

RUBI LOVES SCIENCE AND TECH – IT JUST WORKS... FOR HER, AT LEAST!

HEENA CHANDRA

HARSHA'S BIG SISTER AND THE FASTEST MESSAGE-TYPER IN THE WORLD (PROBABLY).

HARSHA CHANDRA

HARSHA'S ALMOST AS GOOD AT PRANKS AS DENNIS, AND HER DAD OWNS BEANOTOWN'S BEST JOKE SHOP!

AND ALSO SOME GROAN-UPS

JOSH THE POSTIE

JOSH IS A FIRST-CLASS POSTMAN – GEDDIT? HE KNOWS EVERYTHING THERE IS TO KNOW ABOUT EVERYONE IN BEANOTOWN.

THE COLONEL

DENNIS'S NEXT-DOOR NEIGHBOUR AND BEANOTOWN'S GREATEST-EVER SOLDIER (HE SAYS).

Welcome to...
BEANOTOWN!

Beanotown Library. Some say it's Beanotown's tallest building – it has the most stories, you see!

This is where the Menace family lives. Menaces by name, Menaces by nature. At least that's what the neighbours say!

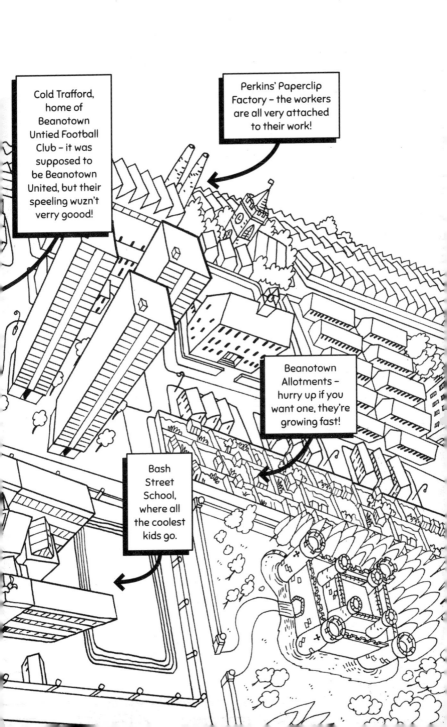

Chapter One

One Catapult To Rule Them All

It was the best catapult Dennis Menace had ever found.

It wasn't a forked branch. It was a forked tree trunk! Dennis dragged his catapult all the way from Beanotown Woods to his house at 51 Gasworks Road.

THIS HAD BETTER BE WORTH IT!

GNEE-HEE!

Dennis's awesome dog Gnasher dug a hole in the lawn. Dennis put the trunk into the hole, then tied a pair of Dad's bum-sculpting elasticated trousers to the fork for elastic.

'Dad won't be happy when he sees what I've done with his trousers,' said Dennis, 'but it will be worth it!'

'Gnash!' said Gnasher. That's what Gnasher says, mostly.

Dennis picked up a sack of rotten tomatoes he'd found in the bins at the back of WIDL (Beanotown's cheapest supermarket), and loaded the yucky, squishy fruit into the seat of the trousers.

He pulled the fully loaded trousers back as far as he could. 'This is going to be the best **SPLAT** in history!' said Dennis. 'Dad's shed won't know what hit it!'

The elastic in the trousers

STRETCHED and **QUIVERED.**

Dennis closed one eye to make sure he was going to score a direct hit on Dad's shed, then let go. Time seemed to slow down.

First, the super-stretched elastic snapped back to normal size, hurling the rotten tomatoes at the shed.

Then the shed door opened and Dad stepped out, newspaper tucked under his arm.

'**Uh-oh!**' said Dennis. 'I didn't check to see if anyone was in there!'

Ninety-nine red tomatoes rocketed towards Dad at the speed of fright.

Dad looked like a giant, surprised, strawberry jelly baby.

Dennis saw the funny side. His baby sister Bea

saw the funny side. Mum saw the funny side.

Dennis's Gran hopped on her motorbike and

came round just to make sure she didn't miss seeing her son covered in smelly tomato pulp.

But grumpy Dad definitely did **not** see the funny side.

'All I'm saying is I'm not sure if grounding him for ten years is enough of a punishment,' raged Dennis Senior.

'Eyes closed!' ordered Mum, aiming the power washer at him.

SHRIEK!

Don't let Mum's face fool you – she's enjoying that! – The Ed

'That's COLD!' whimpered Dad. 'Can't I just go inside and have a nice hot shower?'

'And get tomato juice on my new carpet? No way!' Mum replied, giving him another blast, on the bum this time.

'GNASH-GNASH-GNASH!' said Gnasher, because the postman was at the gate.

'Letter for you,' the postman called, staying firmly outside on the street. 'It's a wedding invitation. Your cousin Lindy's getting married to Marcus in Nuttytown in two weeks.'

'Are you reading our mail again, Josh?' Dad asked.

'Er, no . . . I'm just good at guessing!' said Josh, folding the letter into a paper aeroplane and launching it at Dad's face.

OUCH!

Mum picked up the letter and opened it.

'Aw! You'll never guess . . .' she said, smiling.

'Lindy and Marcus are getting married in
Nuttytown in two weeks?' said Dad.

'Yes!' cried Mum. 'Isn't it exciting? Oh, and
it says grown-ups only – no kids!'

'Yippee!' cried Dad. 'A whole day out on our own with no kids!'

'You don't have to be quite so happy about that,' said Dennis. 'You'll hurt Bea's feelings.'

'So, who's looking after the kids?' asked Gran.

Mum and Dad stared at her.

'Oh! I just thought . . . well, *you*,' said Mum, a little flustered.

'Sorry,' said Gran, reaching inside her jacket and pulling out an envelope identical to the one Mum was holding. 'I've been invited to the wedding too.'

'Oh no,' said Dad. 'This is bad.'

'Really bad,' said Mum. 'We're going to need . . .'

'. . . A BABYSITTER!'

'I don't *need* a babysitter!' objected Dennis. 'They would just ruin a great day in with no groan-ups to bother me!'

'*You* might think you don't need one,' said Mum, already typing on her phone. 'But Bea definitely does, and I won't be able to relax unless there's someone responsible here. I've just posted a "wanted" ad on Twitface,' she said, hitting SEND.

'It's no use,' moaned Dad. 'No one will want to babysit for *us!*'

'Try to be optimistic,' said Mum. 'I didn't say who needed a babysitter!'

'I love it when you're cunning!' said Dad.

PING! went Mum's phone.

PING! PING! PING! PING! PING! PING!

'See? *Lots* of people would like to babysit for us,' said Mum, smiling. 'Be optimistic. That's what I always say!'

'**UUUUURRRGRGGHHHH!!!**' groaned Dennis. 'Babysitters suck!'

Chapter Two

Battle Of The Babysitters

The first would-be babysitter to reply was the Colonel, Dennis's next-door neighbour. He had been in the army and, now he was retired, he spent his time ordering his garden gnomes around. He called them the Gnome Guard.

Mum said he would be perfect as he wouldn't even need a lift home, and arranged a trial run for the very next evening.

ATTENTION! GNIGEL, GET THOSE SHOULDERS BACK! GNICHOLAS, STOP PICKING YOUR NOSE! GNEDDIE, YOUR FLIES ARE UNDONE! AND AS FOR YOU, GNORRIS...

Exactly on time to the very second, the Colonel marched up the path and almost beat the front door down with his cane.

RAT-A-TAT-TAT!

'ATTEN-SHUN!' boomed the Colonel, when Dennis opened the door.

'Mum, the babysitter's here,' Dennis called, putting his fingers in his ears.

'I AM NOT THE BABYSITTER; I AM YOUR COMMANDING OFFICER!' boomed the Colonel.

He boomed quite a lot. In fact, Dennis couldn't remember a time when the Colonel didn't boom.

Mum and Dad hurried out the door, pulling on their coats.

'We'll be back in an hour,' said Mum. 'Let's see how this trial run goes, OK?'

'YES, MA'AM!' boomed the Colonel, slamming the door behind them as they left.

'Don't worry, Bea,' whispered Dennis. 'I've got this.'

When the Colonel turned around, Dennis beckoned him to lean in close.

'I'M YOUR MAN, SIR!' boomed the Colonel. Dennis shushed him.

'I'm your man, sir. Sorry, sir,' whispered the Colonel. His eyes were alight. He hadn't had this much fun since the garden gnome civil war of 2020. 'What are my orders?'

'Listen very carefully,' said Dennis. 'There's a troop of enemy secret agents out in the garden. We need a brave soldier to keep tabs on them.'

'Say no more, sir!' said the Colonel, saluting. 'You can rely on me!'

With that, he tiptoed to the back door, opened it and was gone.

IT'S WORKING!

'Den-den clever,' said Bea admiringly.

'I know,' chuckled Dennis, high-fiving her.

When Mum and Dad got back, it took them an hour to find the Colonel. He was hiding out in Dennis's tree house with mud smeared all over his face and pampas grass tied to his arms and legs to keep him camouflaged.

'Did the Colonel say anything about what he thought he was doing?' Mum asked Dennis, while Dad walked their neighbour home.

'Only something about a secret mission, and then we never saw him again,' said Dennis, not looking up from his video game, *Rise of the Hamsterbots.*

'OK . . .' said Mum, crossing out the

Colonel's name from her list of potential babysitters. 'Who's next?'

'Hello!' the next young woman said. 'I'm **Fabulous Edelweiss.'**

'Hi, Fabulous,' said Mum. 'What an absolutely . . . er, fabulous name! Would you like to come in and meet Dennis and Bea?'

Dennis was crawling around the living room with Bea sitting on his back.

Bea giggled so hard, she toppled from Dennis's back and landed on her head.

'**OWIE!**' she said, pointing to where it was sore. Gnasher licked the spot, and Bea was happy again.

Mmmmmm, Bea's hair tastes like baby food!

'Dennis, Bea, your babysitter is here!' said Mum. 'This is Fabulous.'

'Hello, Den-den and Bea-bea,' simpered Fabulous in a high-pitched baby voice. 'I'm your new best friend, and you are my new best friends. We're all best friends together!'

Something tells me Fabulous is in for a tough evening! – The Ed

'Speaking like that makes them trust me,' said Fabulous to Mum, as though Dennis and Bea couldn't hear her. 'They're in safe hands.'

Mum and Dad left. They were going to *The Hangry Caterpillar*, Beanotown's newest vegan restaurant.

Nobody likes being treated like a baby.
Even Bea, who technically *was* a baby.

'Drawing?' asked Dennis, grinning
mischievously. 'We prefer painting . . .
and decorating!'

Fabulous looked at Dennis, and then Bea.
She had a bad feeling about this . . .

There was no sign of Fabulous when Mum and
Dad got home, but that wasn't the only thing
that was strange.

'Is the living room a different . . . colour?'
asked Mum.

'Fabulous said we could do some painting,'
said Dennis. 'But we thought we'd go the
whole hog and change the wallpaper too.'

21

Dennis wasn't kidding. They'd pulled Mum's wallpaper sample books out of the cupboard, ripped each sample out and used them to paper the walls. And the ceiling. And the door! The effect was . . . overwhelming.

The walls seemed to move in front of Mum's eyes. Actually, the wall *was* moving!

Mum darted across the room and tore
a bulging piece of wallpaper from the wall,
revealing the startled, blinking face of
Fabulous Edelweiss.

THOSE CHILDREN ARE
MONSTERS! LOOK WHAT
THEY DID TO ME!

'I'll get the wallpaper scraper and set
Fabulous free,' sighed Dad.

He just wanted to be out of the room when
Mum started shouting.

But surprisingly Mum wasn't even that mad. She took a deep, steadying breath. She hadn't really liked the colour of the walls anyway, and now she had a great excuse to decorate the living room again.

She scored Fabulous's name off her list.

The hunt for the perfect babysitter went on.

Grizzly Griller said they were the wildest creatures that had ever given him a wedgie.

Sergeant
Slipper said
they were a
'crimewave
with a combined
age of eleven.'

Bananaman took
them with him on
one of his awesome crime-fighting
adventures, which Mum said could have been

dangerous . . .

for the bad

guys!

Mum sighed, defeated. She was at the bottom of her list. There was no one left.

'That's it,' she said. 'Bananaman was our last hope. We can't go to the wedding. There's just no one – not even a superhero – up to the challenge of looking after this pair.'

Dad ruffled Bea's hair, secretly proud because he was quite a lot like her when he'd been a baby.

'Hang on!' said Dennis. 'You mean if we can't find a babysitter, you won't go to the wedding? We won't have a parent-free day?!'

'Of course,' said Mum. 'What did you think would happen?'

'I thought you'd go to the wedding anyway and leave me in charge,' said Dennis. 'What a bummer.'

His brain started to work. There had to be

a solution . . .

And then Dennis grinned.

'I know someone who would be the perfect

babysitter,' he said.

Chapter Three

Brain Of Beanotown

Dennis was generally a doer, not a thinker, but when he tried, he was actually pretty clever.

Mum wanted to know who the mystery babysitter was, but Dennis said to leave it to him. He said Mum and Dad should go to the cinema the next night, and he would arrange the babysitter. They could trust him.

OK, BUT I'M NOT GOING IF I DON'T LIKE THIS BABYSITTER, DENNIS.

STOP TELLING US TO TRUST YOU. IT ONLY MAKES US SUSPICIOUS!

YOU WILL. TRUST ME!

'Who do you think this mystery babysitter is?' Mum asked, as they got ready upstairs the next evening.

'I think it will be that librarian he's always talking about,' said Dad, combing his hair forward so he looked a little younger.

'The one who dresses up as a yeti to make the library more fun?' Mum asked. 'But we've never even actually seen their . . . face!'

Dad thought for a second. 'Butch Butcher?'

Mum shook her head. 'It's the Elvis Presley Impersonators Convention in Las Vegas next Saturday evening. Butch will be watching it online – he never misses it.'

DING-DONG!

'Well, we're about to find out who it is,' said Dad. 'They're here, whoever they are.'

Mum opened the front door to reveal Heena Chandra standing on the doorstep, a nervous smile plastered across her face. Heena's dad owned Har Har's Joke Shop, Beanotown's biggest practical joke and novelty shop.

'Hi, Heena,' smiled Mum. 'Come in!'

'Hi Heena,' said Dennis, sliding down the stair bannister.

'Heena's sixteen, Mum,' said Dennis, 'and very mature.'

'Would you excuse us just for a second, Heena?' said Mum, pushing Dennis and Dad into the kitchen. 'Family conference.'

'Of course,' said Heena, picking up Bea and making a funny face to the baby's delight.

'Well, what do you think?' said Dad, as Mum closed the door.

'She's definitely old enough,' said Mum. 'And the Chandras are a nice family. And she seems good with Bea . . .'

'She's Harsha and Hani's big sister, so she's used to looking after younger people,' said Dennis eagerly.

'I think . . .' said Mum, 'that we should give her a chance.'

'YES!' said Dennis, fist pumping.

'YES!' said Dad, just pumping.

SORRY, IT'S ALL THE EXCITEMENT.

Ten minutes later, Mum and Dad were on their way to Beanotown Cinema to see *Harry Snotter and the Hanky of Secrets,* and Heena was lying on the sofa making good use of the Menaces' Wi-Fi.

The doorbell rang. It was Harsha, Heena's little sister and one of Dennis's best friends. Harsha is a master prankster and always has a scheme up her sleeve.

'Did they fall for it?' Harsha asked when Dennis let her in. 'Your mum and dad didn't know I was coming over?'

'Hook, line and stinker!' he laughed. 'They think me and Bea are having a quiet night in, but actually, the three of us are going to have a great time while Heena does whatever she does on her phone all night. And I'll get a warning on my phone when Mum and Dad get within five minutes of the house, so we'll have plenty of time for you to scarper.'

DOWNLOAD
'PARENT ALARM APP'
NOW
FED UP OF GETTING BUSTED BY YOUR GROAN-UPS? YOU'LL NEVER GET CAUGHT AGAIN IF YOU INSTALL THE 'PARENT ALARM'! GET A WARNING WHENEVER ONE OF YOUR OLDIES COMES NEAR. SET YOUR OWN SAFE SPACE, FROM FIVE METRES TO FIVE MILES! CAN ALSO BE USED ON TEACHERS

'And,' he continued, 'if this works out, you can come over while they're at the wedding for a whole day of parent-free pranking!'

'Listen up, you two!' interrupted Heena, cheerily. 'You know the deal: you don't bother me, I don't bother you. Now scram!'

'What are we waiting for?' chuckled Harsha. 'Let's get this party started!'

This had been Dennis's plan all along. With Heena busy on her phone, he, Harsha and Bea could do whatever they liked for the whole evening.

So long as Harsha was out of the way when Mum and Dad got back, they would never know! Dennis and Harsha got to have fun, and Heena got to earn a bit of money and burn through several terabytes of free

Wi-Fi instead of using her own phone data.

WIN-WIN!

Dennis picked up Bea and the three of them headed upstairs to play Fartnite, listen to music, eat snacks and have a laugh. It was great. No one told them to get their pyjamas on, be quiet, stop stomping on the floor, not to ride tea trays down the stairs or put Mum and Dad's clothes on Gnasher.

At half past ten, Dennis's phone buzzed.

'That's my Parent Alarm!' he said. 'We've got five minutes to tidy up and get you out the back door.'

They rushed around the house, tidying up, putting clothes away, putting Bea to bed and throwing the dishes into the sink (luckily, they were plastic and didn't break).

When Dennis heard the scratching of Mum's key in the front door, Harsha sneaked out of the back door and into the garden.

'Wait out here for Heena and she can walk you home,' said Dennis, then he shut the door.

'Hi Mum!' said Dennis, cheerily. 'Good timing! Bea's sleeping and I just finished reading my book.'

He waved his copy of *The Complete Encyclopedia of Completely Everything* by Dr. Hugh Mungus-Brayne.

'Crumbs!' said Dad. 'I've had that book since I was your age, and I *still* haven't finished it!'

WELL, HEENA? WAS EVERYTHING OK?

YES, EVERYTHING WAS FINE. THEY WERE AS GOOD AS GOLD.

'Well,' said Mum, when she'd shown Heena out. 'I think that was a successful evening. No phone calls from angry firemen or neighbours with flooded gardens. Heena said you were both very good, and the house is still in one piece!'

'So, what about the wedding?' asked Dennis eagerly, thinking about a whole day of freedom from his parents.

Mum took out her phone.

'What are you doing?' asked Dad.

'Looking online for a hat to wear,' said Mum, smiling to herself.

Dennis grinned. His plan had worked. He couldn't wait for the weekend to come!

Chapter Four

Wedding Distress

Mum and Dad slept in on the day of the wedding because Dennis had crept in during the night and put their alarm clock in a bowl of jelly, and they were now in a huge rush to get ready.

'We're going to be late,' cried Mum, running down the stairs three at a time.

'I can't remember how to tie my tie,' said Dad, who would have done a better job if he hadn't also been trying to brush his teeth at the same time.

OW! MY EARS! MY NOSE!

LET ME HELP!

Dad rubbed his ears. All he could hear was a loud rumbling sound.

'Gran's here!' called Dennis.

Gran threw open the front door and stomped in wearing her black motorbike leathers.

'Is that what you're wearing to the wedding?' Dad asked, horrified. 'We don't have time for you to get changed!'

HELLO, GRAN-FANS!

Gran smirked and laid her helmet on the table. She thrust a hand into her pocket and pulled out a rose, which she pinned to her chest.

'There!' she said. 'I'm ready now!'

Dennis laughed. Gran was awesome!

'Hello?' came a voice from the door.

'Hi, Heena!' said Dad. 'In you come!'

Mum handed Heena a sheet of paper.

'Everything you need should be on here,' she said. 'I've written down my mobile number, Dad's number, Gran's number, the number of the hotel, the number of the bride and the number of the vicar. Someone should pick up. And I've written down a few little dos and don'ts.'

'Everything will be fine,' Heena smiled, looking at the list. There were far more than a few dos and don'ts . . .

DO put Bea down for a nap in the afternoon

DO make sure Dennis puts his laundry away

DO ask Dennis to put the breakfast dishes in the dishwasher

DO sniff Bea's bottom every half an hour or so

DON'T give Dennis the key to the shed – the ladder is in there

DON'T let Dennis play DEATH FOOTY 5: EXTRA TIME

DON'T let Dennis pretend to be the mayor and order takeaway for the town hall

DON'T let them out of your sight (or earshot) – that's when things get hairy

'We really have to go, Sandra,' said Dad.

Mum gave Bea a hug and Dennis a big wet slobbery kiss on the cheek. 'Be good, I love you, see you later,' she said, blowing more kisses as Dad ushered her out of the door.

'Ugh! MU-Um!' said Dennis, wiping his cheek.

The front door closed, and for a moment

the Menace house was quiet. Bea looked at Gnasher. Gnasher looked at Dennis. This was very odd.

The back door opened. Gnasher growled. Who was this?

HI, PALS!
IT'S ONLY ME!

Gnice to see you, Harsha!

'OK,' said Heena. 'Can we go over the rules, please? You guys leave me alone unless you need to use the cooker or there's an emergency.

In return, I won't tell anyone that I let you come over to play, Harsha. Deal?'

'Deal,' said Dennis and Harsha together. Bea clapped her hands.

Heena headed for one of the comfy chairs in the living room, leaving Dennis, Gnasher, Harsha and Bea standing alone in the hallway, with twelve glorious hours of no-groan-up freedom stretching out in front of them.

'What do you want to do first?' Dennis asked excitedly.

'Funny you should say that,' said Harsha, taking off her backpack. 'My dad gave me some new pranks he wants us to test out. If you're up for it, that is.'

WHEN HAVE I EVER NOT BEEN UP FOR ANYTHING?!

They crept around the outside of the house and into the back garden. From Dennis's jungle of a yard, they could see into the Colonel's immaculately groomed garden. Everything was perfect. The grass had edges that looked like they'd been drawn with a ruler. The flowers all stood up perfectly straight. Even the birds seemed to fly in formation, like a display team of jet fighters. The Colonel was outside in his garden, barking orders at his gnomes.

Harsha pulled a clockwork rat out of her rucksack and handed it to Dennis. He turned the key to wind the mechanism.

'This will really wind him up!' Dennis whispered through his giggles.

Dennis set the rat down on the Colonel's side of the fence and ducked out of sight. The rat whizzed onto the lawn, right in front of the Colonel, but instead of travelling in a straight line, it zoomed all over the place, turning left, right, speeding up and slowing down. It even squeaked occasionally.

'YOU THERE!' said the Colonel, pointing at the rat. 'HOW DARE YOU BREAK RANKS, YOU 'ORRIBLE LITTLE TOERAG!'

MUTINY! HOW DARE YOU ATTACK A FELLOW SOLDIER!

Eek! Gnome down! – The Ed

The Colonel waved his stick at the other gnomes. 'GET THE TRAITOR, MEN!'

The gnomes did nothing. The rat spun to the left, then to the right, then shot straight towards the Colonel.

'HE'S ATTACKING THE COMMANDING OFFICER!' the Colonel shrieked. 'I HAVE NEVER SEEN SUCH INSUBORDINATION!'

The Colonel backed away from the advancing rat, which was, in his opinion, now squeaking at him in a very aggressive manner.

'YOU'LL BE COURT-MARTIALLED!' he yelled, still stepping backwards.

From their hiding place, the pals watched gleefully as the drama unfolded.

'He's forgotten about his pond!' said Harsha, stifling her laughter.

The Colonel took one more step backwards, his foot feeling helplessly for solid ground where there was none.

The Colonel hit the water like an elephant falling off a jet ski. The splash was so big, a few drops landed on Gnasher.

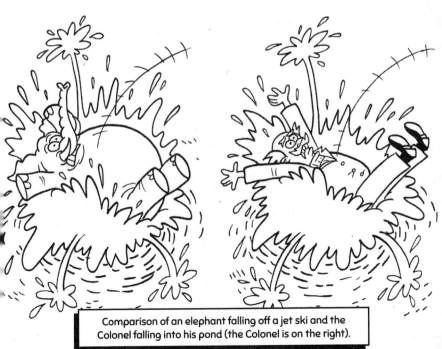

Comparison of an elephant falling off a jet ski and the Colonel falling into his pond (the Colonel is on the right).

'**GNASH!**' said Gnasher delightedly.

The Colonel hauled himself out using the fishing line held by one of his faithful gnomes.

The clockwork rat trundled back to the fence, slowing down. Dennis reached through and grabbed it.

'Come on,' he said. 'Before the Colonel dries out and spots us!'

They dashed back to the Menace house, holding their laughter in until the door was safely closed.

BWA-HA-HA-HA!

They laughed endlessly, tears rolling down their cheeks.

'Did you see how angry he was with the rat?' asked Dennis, wiping tears from his eyes.

'I know,' said Harsha, 'and what about when he was "rescued" by that gnome with the fishing rod?'

Bea giggled and made splashing noises, but suddenly sat down and yawned.

'Bea needs a nap,' said Dennis. 'Let's take her upstairs.'

When Bea was snoring in her cot, Dennis and Harsha tiptoed quietly out of her room and into Dennis's.

'We can play on my Nontendo until Bea wakes up, then have some more fun,' said Dennis.

I'VE GOT A BETTER IDEA... IF YOU'RE BRAVE ENOUGH!

Chapter Five

Sister Act

'You want to prank Heena?' said Dennis, disbelieving. 'She'll call my parents!'

'No, she won't,' said Harsha. 'Heena is happy – my parents aren't disturbing her and she's got free Wi-Fi. Even if she gets mad, she won't want to ruin her whole day.'

BUT WHAT IF YOU'RE WRONG?

'What do you think, Gnasher?'

Dennis asked.

GNASH-GNASH-GNASH!
I think it's a big risk.
If she flips her biscuit
and calls Mum and Dad,
YOU'RE TOAST!

'OK,' said Dennis. 'Gnasher thinks it's a good idea. I'm in.'

I can smell trouble a mile away, thought Gnasher, heading for the gnash-flap in the kitchen door. *I'm off to the tree house for a gnash-gnap!*

'I've got a prank I've been saving for a special occasion,' said Harsha.

※ ※ ※

Heena was messaging her friend Steph on WotSlap, who was having an argument with her boyfriend on Instaslam.

Steph is typing . . . her phone told her.

'Hurry up, Steph!' Heena grumbled.

She was so absorbed in Steph's argument that she didn't see the hand reach around the cushion of the chair she was sitting on. She didn't see the airhorn it was holding either. And she definitely didn't see the hand holding another airhorn that reached around from the other side . . .

Miraculously, the **HONK** didn't wake Bea from her nap. However, the **THUMP** of Heena hitting the floor certainly did.

Bea rubbed her eyes. There was no one in her room, but she could hear laughter coming from downstairs.

She grabbed the top rail of the cot and, like a tiny ninja, swung herself up and over it.

Uh-oh! thought Bea, as she realised it was quite a long way down to the floor . . .

Luckily, Bea was an expert in tiny ninja landings, so her nappy took most of the impact.

She picked herself up and set off in the direction of the stairs.

THUDDITY-THUDDITY-CRUMP-WHACK-THUDDITY!

That was the sound Bea made as she tiny-ninja-rolled down the stairs.

There was a lot of shouting coming from the living room. She stuck her head around the door to see what was happening.

Dennis and Harsha were rolling around on the floor, laughing helplessly.

'Did you see her face?' cackled Harsha. 'Har har!'

'No,' giggled Dennis, 'but I filmed the whole thing on my phone!'

Heena angrily got back to her feet, waving her phone at them.

'Really, Dennis? You'll be sorry when I phone your parents and tell them about your and Harsha's little plan!'

'You're not going to do that, Heena,' said Harsha calmly. 'First, you're loving being out of the house with free Wi-Fi and no adults to cramp your style. Second, you're getting paid for this. And third, you were in on this plan too, so it's not just us you're dobbing in!'

Heena scowled. Harsha was right. She'd get in trouble too!

Bea reversed into the hallway. It didn't look like a lot of fun in there. She remembered the funny man falling into the pond earlier. That *was* fun, but that had been outside and the front door was closed.

She investigated the kitchen. The back door was closed too.

But the flap Gnasher used to come in and out hadn't been shut properly . . .

Bea crawled through the kitchen, pushed the gnash-flap open and crawled out.

She crawled round the side of the house, down the garden path and out of the gate. She looked left, then she looked right. The shouting from the living room was still loud and it still didn't sound like fun. And the whole, exciting world was out here, right in front of her.

But where to go?

Bea's tummy rumbled and gave her an idea.

RUMBLE

Chapter Six

Mobile Phun

QUI-I-I-I-ET!

Dennis and Harsha were silent.

'All this shouting does no good for anyone,'
Heena carried on, breathing heavily. 'Here's the

deal: you two leave me alone, or I call Mr and Mrs Menace and we all get in trouble.'

Dennis put up his hand as if Heena was a teacher. 'If we leave *you* alone, will you leave *us* alone?'

'Absolutely!' said Heena.

'**DEAL!**' said Harsha and stretched out a hand. 'Shake on it!'

But when Heena reached out to take her hand . . .

'Come on, Harsha,' giggled Dennis. 'Let's go before Heena changes her mind.'

They went upstairs to Dennis's room to continue their pranks in peace. When they got to the landing, Harsha stopped and listened at Bea's bedroom door.

SILENCE!

'Literally sleeping like a baby,' said Harsha. 'Come on, let's have some phone fun!'

Harsha dialled a number on Dennis's phone and handed it to him. When Butch Butcher answered, Dennis said, in his best Mayor Brown voice, 'Butch Butcher? This is Mayor Brown. I'd like to make a complaint.'

'Really?' Butch replied. 'Have you got a beef with my beef?'

'No,' said Dennis. 'But the turkey you

sold me won't come out of the fridge. It's just trembling and it says it's scared.'

'So what?' said Butch.

'Well, that turkey you sold me is clearly a chicken!'

Dennis hung up and burst out laughing. He handed the phone back to Harsha, who dialled another number.

'One more,' said Harsha, stifling her laughter and grabbing the phone again.

'It's Mr Ring's doughnut shop,' she whispered to Dennis as he listened to the phone ringing.

'Ah, is that Mr Ring?' asked Dennis. 'This is your mayor. I ordered six doughnuts this morning and I am horrified to discover that there are holes in every one of them. HOLES, I tell you!'

'Gosh!' said Mr Ring. 'But all my doughnuts have holes in them, Mr Mayor!'

Dennis hung up, unable to hold his laughter in any longer.

Dennis and Harsha lay back on Dennis's bed, cackling. Harsha's phone buzzed. It was a message from Heena downstairs.

Dennis crept across the landing to check on Bea. It was still quiet. *Bea must have been tired*, he thought. *She's having a long nap!*

He slowly pushed the door open, and . . .

Dennis shut the door, waited for a second, then opened it again and looked in. Then he ran back to his bedroom.

'B-B-Bea!' he stammered. 'G-g-gone!'

'Gone potty-poo-poo, has she?' chuckled Harsha. 'How bad is the smell?'

'No, she's *gone*,' said Dennis. 'She's not in her bedroom!'

'What? Are you sure? She can't be far away,' said Harsha. 'She's just a baby.'

They checked Bea's room thoroughly.

Then Dennis's room.

BEA?

Then they checked the bathroom because
Bea liked to sniff the air freshener in the toilet.

Then under the stairs (Dennis knew she
wouldn't be in there because she was scared of
the vacuum cleaner).

Then the kitchen.

'What about the living room?' said Dennis. 'We'll have to tell Heena though.'

'She'll only freak out,' said Harsha.

But Bea was nowhere else in the house. They decided to risk checking the living room, pretending that Dennis had left his phone somewhere so Heena wouldn't get suspicious while they frantically checked behind the sofa cushions.

'We've looked everywhere,' groaned Dennis. 'Where can she be?'

'She has to be in the house,' said Harsha. 'The doors are all shut and she isn't tall enough to reach the handles.'

Just then, a sleepy-looking Gnasher appeared through the gnash-flap in the kitchen door.

Dennis looked at Gnasher, then at the baby-sized gnash-flap, then at Harsha.

'She would fit through there,' he said.

'OMG!' said Harsha.

'You don't think . . .' he said.

'I don't know,' said Harsha, 'but it's possible.'

Dennis knelt beside Gnasher, who was still groggy from his gnash-nap.

'I need you to find Bea, Gnasher,' Dennis said. 'It's really important!'

Gnasher sniffed the air. The wiry, black toilet brush Gnasher called a tail traced a circular motion in the air. Dennis and Harsha held their breath. Suddenly, the tail went stiff and pointed like an arrow . . . straight out of the gnash-flap!

'*We* can use the door, silly!' said Dennis, yanking the handle down and heading out into the fresh air. Gnasher was already at the gate, nose to the ground. **SNUFFLE!**

He looked right – snuffled – then left – another snuffle. And then . . .

Gnasher dashed off down Gasworks Road. Dennis and Harsha followed.

'I'm thinking,' said Dennis as they ran. 'Bea hasn't had her lunch yet, so she might have gone for something to eat.'

'What does she like?' asked Harsha.

'The thing about Bea is that even though she's little, she has a massive sweet tooth,' said Dennis. 'I bet she's gone to the sweet shop!'

'I'll call Rubi,' said Harsha, pulling out her phone. 'She lives near the sweet shop. Maybe she can help!'

Calling
Rubi . . .

Chapter Seven

The Sweetie Shack

The Sweetie Shack is Beanotown's biggest sweet shop. It likes to claim it has a sweet for absolutely everyone.

Sweets for vegetarians, sweets for vegans,

halal sweets, sweets for people with allergies . . .
They even have sweets for people who don't
like sweets (even though that's basically a
carrot stick).

Bea has three favourite sweets. She likes
Yucky Yetis from the Gumalayas and Sticky
Strawberry Burps, but today what she really,
really wanted was a Fumey the Flaming
Fumicorn's Exploding Butt. Fumey the Flaming
Fumicorn is an angry unicorn
who's furious because
his delicious, chewy
bottom is always
exploding.

YES, I AM FURIOUS.
AND YES, MY BUTT
DOES EXPLODE . . .
WITH SHERBET!

There are lots of ways to eat an FFFEB. You start with the gummy, blackcurrant-flavoured, outer part. You can chew it, lick it, suck it, gnaw it, chomp it or nibble it. You can take it out of your mouth, stick it behind your ear and put it back in your mouth again.

If you keep doing all of these things for long enough, you will eventually make a tiny hole in Fumey's blackcurrant bottom.

This will make Fumey's butt explode, and you will be rewarded with a fizzy shot of sugary sherbet, which will flow right up the back of your nose, out of your nostrils and all over your clean clothes.

Strictly speaking, this isn't a sensible sweet to give a one-year-old, but Dad liked to sneak Bea sweets when he had the kids by himself. And who was he to deny his darling daughter an Exploding Butt?

Bea knew exactly where to get herself an Exploding Butt. She hopped on the bottom of a shopping trolley and used it like a giant baby stroller. As she turned from the Gooey Gross-Out section into Mythical Creature Land, she kicked over a display of Giant Gob-stoppers, the longest-lasting sweet ever invented.

GIANT GOB-STOPPERS

WHOOPSIES!

There are old-age pensioners who have spent their whole lives eating their first Giant Gob-stopper. They sucked it all day, took it out (possibly along with their teeth) at night, and started sucking again in the morning.

Bea giggled as the long-lasting lickables rolled across the shop floor in all directions.

A woman carrying a dozen chocolate eggs stood on one, which was a bit of a surprise, to say the least. She threw the eggs into the air and fell into the fudge fridge. Then the eggs landed on her head.

A man browsing for fruit chews fell backwards into the bubblegum ball pit and disappeared beneath the sweets.

One man who trod on two Giant Gob-stoppers didn't fall over, but rolled – at 32.7 miles an hour, to be precise – into the candy floss display.

The giant bag of candy floss burst as he hit it, spun sugar erupting out of it like a car airbag going off. Miraculously, he didn't break any bones, but he did have a loud ringing in his ears and had to walk home with every dog in Beanotown trying to lick him clean.

FOOM!

OOF! THE PAIN IS...
KIND OF SWEET?

Bea hopped off her shopping trolley when she reached her destination. She looked up, past the Super Sugar Magic Mermaids, past the Loch Sticky Mess Monsters and even past the Kandy Krakens.

Finally, right on the very top shelf, she saw what she had come for: Fumey and his fizzy exploding bottom.

Fearless little Bea started to climb up!

Outside, Gnasher, Dennis and Harsha were just arriving, thanks to Gnasher's gnifty gnose. As they burst through the doors of The Sweetie Shack, they scanned the shop for Bea.

'**Look**!' cried Dennis, pointing to a security monitor on the wall. On the screen, Bea was scaling the shelves, while lots of grown-ups seemed to be throwing themselves on the ground. Weird. But Harsha had spotted something even worse . . .

'**Oh no**!' she said. 'Mrs Creecher's in Creepy-Crawly Alley!'

Mrs Creecher is the headteacher at Bash Street School, where Dennis, Harsha and all the cool kids in Beanotown go. Mrs Creecher knows Dennis's parents very, VERY well. I wonder why?

'If she spots Bea out all alone, my mum and dad will find out about it for sure!' said Dennis. **'Come on!'**

Dennis, Gnasher and Harsha sprinted into the shop and expertly dodged the groaning grown-ups, slithering staff and – most of important of all – the helpless headteacher!

But, as they skidded around the corner into Mythical Creature Land, they froze!

Bea was hanging from the top shelf, her little legs kicking and tears springing from her eyes.

HELP, DEN–DEN!

'She's going to fall!' shouted Dennis.
'Go, Gnasher!'

Dennis's faithful Abyssinian wire-haired tripe hound stuck out his claws for extra grip and sped towards Bea, whose fingers were beginning to slip. She squealed in horror as she lost her grip entirely and started to fall.

Gnasher launched himself into the air and used his back to flip Bea up and onto the top shelf like a bucking bronco flips a cowboy. Bea

landed on her bottom, right beside Fumey the
Flaming Fumicorn!

Gnasher breathed a big sigh of doggy relief,
then realised he hadn't thought about where
he was going to land.

KERRRASH!

Gnasher crashed into the shelves, knocking them over like a massive domino rally!

CRASH! THUMP! WALLOP! BOOM!

One after another the shelves toppled to the floor. Dennis watched through his fingers in horror as the shelf Bea was

sitting on started

to wobble and

fall over . . .

As the shelf sloped downwards, the baby slid gracefully to the edge, then tumbled off and out of sight.

'**BEA!**' cried Dennis.

They ran to the end of the aisle, fearing the worst. But there was no Bea, just a big display of Mega Marshmallow Pillows (the sweet you always dream of eating).

'Where is she?' said Harsha, puzzled.

'I don't know,' said Dennis. 'She must have landed in these Marshmallow Pillows, the lucky thing!'

'Gnash-gnash!' barked Gnasher furiously. He was following a trail of sticky hand and knee prints that led right out of The Sweetie Shack's automatic doors. Dennis ran after Gnasher, and Harsha would have done too,

if a cold hand hadn't gripped her by
the shoulder.

'I think you should help clear up this mess,
Miss Chandra,' said Mrs Creecher sternly.
'Don't you?'

Harsha nodded, glumly.

Outside, Bea wondered what she should do
with herself next. The sweet shop had been
fun, but there'd been a lot of angry grown-up

shouting going on, which she didn't like. She spotted a little black dog being lifted into the back of a car by an elderly man surrounded by shopping bags.

'Gnash-gnash!' chuckled Bea, climbing into the car to say hello while the man put his shopping in the boot. But, before she could even take a good look at the dog, the man had shut the boot, closed the back door and climbed into the driver's seat.

'Jings, Hamish!' said the man, firing up the engine. 'We're a wee bit late!'

Bea looked at Hamish. He wasn't Gnasher after all, but he looked friendly and he had a moustache that looked exactly like his owner's! Bea patted him on the head. Hamish licked her on the cheek.

The old man jammed the car into gear and screeched out into the traffic. Bea looked out of the window, just in time to see Dennis and Gnasher coming out of The Sweetie Shack. She waved. She saw Dennis look back at her and shout something she couldn't hear. Then they were gone.

Bea yawned, lay down on the seat beside her new friend and shut her eyes.

Chapter Eight

Rubi To The Rescue

'Creecher's got Harsha,' Dennis said to Gnasher, as they dashed out of The Sweetie Shack's doors. 'Normally, I'd go back to save her, but I've got to find Bea!'

A green car screeched away from the kerb. Dennis was going to give the driver his best

'Hey, there might be kids playing around here!' glare, but then he noticed two little faces looking out of the rear window. One of the faces belonged to a cute little black dog with a moustache, and the other was . . .

'BEA!' yelled Dennis. 'HEY, BEA!'

Bea waved back, and then the car was gone.

Dennis wanted to scream. He'd been so close to finding his little sister, but now he had no idea how to get to her.

SCREECH!

Rubi Von Screwtop skidded to a stop millimetres from the big toe on Dennis's right foot.

'Harsha explained everything,' said Rubi. 'Well, everything up to you losing Bea and then following her to The Sweetie Shack. But now you're out here and Harsha is nowhere to be seen, so I guess something else has happened.'

Dennis really quickly filled Rubi in on the latest events.

Rubi is super intelligent and a genius with science, gadgets and stuff like thinking. Dennis is good at thinking too, but his thinking bits usually get to work after his doing bits have made a mess of everything.

Rubi does her thinking first, which Dennis always means to try but never remembers in time. She had a plan in five seconds flat.

'Hop on,' she ordered. Dennis climbed onto the back of her chair, which had stunt pegs in case she ever needed to give anyone a lift. Gnasher climbed onto Dennis's back and clung on.

Rubi pressed a button on her control pad and a little drone buzzed out of a hatch on her chair. It shot into the air and set off after the car with Bea in it.

Rubi pressed another button, this time marked MAX SPEED, and her chair sped after the drone.

'My camera drone will find and track the car,' she called back to Dennis. 'And it's connected to Beanotown Maps, so it will control my chair until we catch up.'

'You mean the chair is driving and not you?' gulped Dennis.

'Don't worry,' chuckled Rubi. 'I am driving, really. Well, I programmed it. It's perfectly safe.'

They hurtled down Parkins Crescent, where a man was admiring a repair he'd done to the pavement with quick-drying cement. A queue of people waiting for a bus looked on appreciatively.

Rubi's chair sprayed the man and the queue with cement, and before they could say 'I thought this sort of thing only happened in comics?' they found themselves trapped in rock-hard concrete.

SORRY! IT'S NOT LIKE WE CE–MEANT THAT TO HAPPEN!

SPLURCH!

They rounded the corner onto Beanotown High Street. Butch Butcher was carrying a long string of sausages from his shop to his van.

'Look out, Butch!' yelled Dennis.

'YIKES!' cried Butch, jumping out of the way just in time.

A swerve and a duck, and they made it safely past.

'Phew!' said Rubi. 'That was close!'

'Gnom-gnom!' said Gnasher, who'd grabbed the end of Butch's enormous string of sausages and was gulping it down one banger at a time. Unfortunately for Butch, he was still holding the other end and being spun round and round like a spinning top. When the last sausage slipped from his grasp, he fell over, as dizzy as a wombat in a washing machine.

Rubi checked her tablet, which showed where the car was.

'We're gaining on Bea,' she said.

'Tomato!' answered Dennis.

'What's tomato?' she asked, puzzled.

'We're about to pile right through a mountain of rotten veg,' said Dennis. 'That's what's the matter!'

He was right. Veg Dwight, Beanotown's greenest greengrocer, was piling boxes and boxes of over-ripe tomatoes outside on sale. Shoppers were crowding round, trying to snap up a bargain.

We can't go over it,' said Rubi, gritting her teeth.

'We can't go under it,' said Dennis, shutting his eyes.

We have to go THROUGH it! thought Gnasher.

SPLAT! SPLAT! SPLAT! SPLAT! SPLAT! SPLAT! SPLAT! SPLAT! SPLAT! SPLAT!

An explosion of tomato juice painted the shoppers, the shop and the shopkeeper bright red.

DON'T WORRY – IT'S ALL ORGANIC!

Rubi inspected her clothes. They were clean. 'Amazing!' she cried. 'We must be going faster than the speed of tomato!'

Meanwhile, in the car, Bea was doing something. Her little face frowned, her nose scrunched up to one side, and then she relaxed.

AHHH... DAT'S BETTER. BEA WENT BOOM-BOOM!

And that's when the smell hit.

'Crivvens, Hamish!' cried the driver. 'Ah'm gonnae huv to change yer dug food! That is mingin'!'

It wisnae me, thought Hamish. *It was the wee bairn!*

'It's nae good,' sighed the man. 'I'm pullin' ower and openin' the doors! Help ma Boab!'

The car pulled over to the kerb, and the man climbed out, coughing and spluttering into his hanky.

He ran around the car, opening the doors, then retreated to a safe distance. Bea patted Hamish on the head and climbed out of the car.

Where am I? she wondered.

※ ※ ※

'BeanoLand!' cried Rubi, waving her tablet at Dennis. 'Bea's car stopped moving, right outside BeanoLand!'

'You're amazing!' cried Dennis. 'Burn rubber, Rubes!'

But instead of going even faster, Rubi's chair started to slow down.

'**Uh-oh!**' she said. 'I'm out of battery. You don't get far at maximum speed.'

'BeanoLand is just round the corner – so go on without me!' said Rubi, pressing a button

on the control panel. A solar panel rose from the back of the chair and unfolded itself over her head.

'I don't want to leave you,' said Dennis, 'but I have to find Bea!'

DON'T WORRY ABOUT ME – MY SOLAR CHARGER WILL GET ME GOING IN NO TIME, AND IT KEEPS THE SUN OFF TOO!

YOU'RE A GENIUS, RUBI – THANK YOU!

BeanoLand was busy. Dennis realised it wasn't going to be easy to find his little sis.

'**Gnash! Gnash-gnash!**' Gnasher yapped excitedly, his nose sniffing the air.

'What's that?' asked Dennis. But Gnasher was already off and running through the crowd at top speed. He'd picked up Bea's scent again and no wonder! Phooey!

'There She is!' cried Dennis, spotting Bea crawling to the front of the queue for the Ghost Train.

'And there she isn't!' he groaned, when Bea disappeared into the darkness of his favourite (until now) fairground ride.

I'VE GOT TO GET TO HER BEFORE THE GHOST TRAIN SCARES HER INTO NEXT YEAR!

THE HOUSE
OF FUN

THE HELTER SKELTER

COLD
DOGS

THE LITTLE WHEEL

THE BIG WHEEL

Chapter Nine

Scream Team

By the time Dennis and Gnasher got to the Ghost Train, it was fully loaded with people looking forward to the fright of their lives.

'And away we go!' cackled the steward, cranking the big handle that started the ride.

The train jolted and started to move, the passengers giggling nervously.

'Stop the ride!' shouted Dennis to the steward. 'My baby sister is in there!'

The steward gasped and tried to wrench the handle into the STOP position, but it broke off in his hands. 'Come on,' the steward shouted, opening a door marked STAFF ONLY. Dennis followed him through it.

Inside the fairground ride, it was pitch black and deathly quiet, apart from the sound of someone . . . giggling.

TEE-HEE-HEE!
DIS IS FUNNY!

'That's Bea,' said Dennis. 'Follow that giggling noise!'

The steward led the way, stepping carefully over the many levers and wires that made the ride work.

'This is the worst ghost train ever,' Dennis said to Gnasher. 'Nothing's happening!'

'The scares only operate when the train gets close and triggers them,' said the steward. 'We'll be fine as long as we don't touch any . . .'

Dennis suddenly spotted an innocent-looking switch lit up by a red light.

CAUTION!
THIS WILL LAUNCH THE SCARES!

DO NOT PRESS!

OK, so it wasn't innocent-looking at all.

Dennis pressed it. Immediately, he could hear mechanical whirring and creaking noises.

'What did you do?' the steward whispered. 'You didn't press the switch that tests all the scares, did you?'

'No,' Dennis fibbed.

A werewolf dummy howled as it jumped out from the wall of the ride, its paws clawing towards the steward. The werewolf glowed bright green in the UV lights that had come on.

'It's not real, dude,' said Dennis.

The lights went off again. Something swished past, coldly brushing against Dennis's cheek. What could that be?

The lights came on again, revealing a vampire flying through the air, straight at the poor steward.

The steward stepped back into the arms of an Egyptian mummy, who hugged him close.

The lights went out again. The steward shrieked again.

'Have you never been on this ride?' asked Dennis. 'I knew what was coming and I don't even work here!'

'There's something hairy now . . .' moaned the steward, 'with huge fangs . . . and a . . . a big, wet, slobbery tongue?!'

'**Gnash-gnash!**' said the latest monster, giving the game away.

'Shh! Be quiet,' said Dennis. 'I thought I heard something.'

They listened. And listened. And . . .

BLARRRRT!

The steward screamed (again). The lights came up and there, so close to his nose that his eyes had to cross to focus, was Bea's bottom.

HA-HA! BEA DID BIG BOOM-BOOM!

Bea giggled, dropped to the floor and crawled away. *Best. Ride. Ever!* she thought. *It was awesome!*

She crawled out of the Ghost Train and chuckled at the people waiting for their turn. They looked nervous. Then, when the train finally emerged from the ride, its passengers were green and choking.

'The smell!' they moaned.

'Me did that!' said Bea proudly.

Then the steward ran straight through the front wall of the ride . . . and kept going!

He ran out of BeanoLand, over Beano Bridge, round Loch Mess and was last seen near the top of Mount Beano. Poor chap!

Bea didn't like the way her nappy felt now. It was heavy and it was getting harder for her to move around. So when she saw a woman carrying another smelly baby at arms' length, she crawled after her.

BeanoLand is the only theme park in the world to have a Patented Automatic Nappy Installation & Cleaning Station (P.A.N.I.C. Station, for short).

Rubi's dad, Professor Von Screwtop, invented it about ten years ago, when Rubi was a baby, but he'd always enjoyed having a laugh and a joke with Rubi while he changed her, so he sold it to BeanoLand.

Now people can put their stinky kids into a human car wash and enjoy a nice coffee while their babies are cleaned and changed.

The woman popped her baby into a little seat and pressed a button, which started the process. Bea pulled the woman's leg and looked up at her with big baby eyes.

'**Phewy!**' said the woman. 'Smells like you could do with a rinse too!'

She popped Bea into the next seat and pressed the button again. The safety bar clicked into place, and Bea's seat began to move, climbing into the open mouth of the automatic nappy changer.

'Bea!' cried Dennis, charging through the crowd toward the P.A.N.I.C. Station. 'Wait up!'

DENNIS'S BEST BABY JOKES!

WHAT SHOULD YOU NEVER FORGET WHEN YOU CHANGE A NAPPY?
NOSE PLUGS!

WHY WAS THERE NO POO IN THE NAPPY?
THE FART BLEW IT AWAY!

WHY DID DAD BUY MILLIONS OF NAPPIES?
HE WANTED TO CHANGE THE WORLD!

WHAT DO YOU PUT ON A PIGLET WITH NAPPY RASH?
OINKMENT!

WHY WAS THE CLEVER NAPPY CONFUSED?
THEY'D ALWAYS BEEN TOP OF THE CLASS IN NAPPY SCHOOL, BUT NOW THEY WERE RIGHT AT THE BOTTOM!

WHY SHOULD YOU BE POLITE WHEN YOU CHANGE A NAPPY?
YOU DON'T WANT TO PUT YOUR FOOT IN IT!

WHAT KIND OF MUSIC DO BABIES LIKE BEST?
POOP MUSIC!

Gnasher sped up and dashed ahead. He knew Dennis couldn't run as fast as him. He reached the P.A.N.I.C. Station and jumped, sticking out a claw to snag Bea with . . . and missed.

'**GNOUCH!**' said Gnasher, as he landed in the next empty seat.

GNUH-OH! thought Gnasher as the safety bar clicked into place, trapping him. **Oh well,** he thought. **I don't know where I'm going, but at least I can keep an eye on Bea from here!**

Dennis arrived at the P.A.N.I.C. Station just in time to see Gnasher disappear inside. There was a terrible **WAIL** and a **GNASH** and a **HOWL** and then, from the clean-baby hatch, Bea appeared, giggling and pointing at Dennis, and looking remarkably clean.

Poor Gnasher! – The Ed

Dennis lifted his little sister from the chair and gave her a big hug.

'I'm never letting you out of my sight again,' he said.

The clean-baby hatch opened again and, with an ear-splitting **'GNYAROO-HOO-HOO,'** Gnasher appeared.

Well, it *sounded* like Gnasher.

Only this Gnasher was fluffy, had a lovely

123

yellow bow around its neck, and was wearing
a nappy.

The gnew Gnasher whimpered. When the
safety bar was released, he scrambled out of
the seat and ran to Dennis. Dennis put Bea
down and consoled his hairy BFF.

I have gnever been so humilia+ed!

'What have they done to you, buddy?'
asked Dennis. Gnasher tore the bow tie from
around his neck and shook himself violently.

'That's better!' said Dennis. 'You look a bit
more like yourself now, Gnasher.'

Gnasher shook himself again, even more vigorously, until his coat sprang out into his old spiky style with a loud PYOING! The real Gnasher was back!

FEELING BETTER, PAL? I THOUGHT I'D FOUND BEA AND LOST YOU FOR A MINUTE THERE! RIGHT, BEA?

There was no answer.

'Bea?' said Dennis again, turning round with a horrible, empty feeling in his tummy.

Bea was gone.

Again.

Chapter Ten

I Love Zoo

Dennis and Gnasher ran back to the BeanoLand entrance and found themselves surrounded by hundreds of penguins.

Yes, real *penguins*!

Every day at 2pm the penguins from Beanotown Zoo go for a walk around the zoo and even out into the streets of the town. It's called the Penguin Parade and is designed to make people want to visit the zoo. Before settling on the penguins, the zoo tried the same idea with other animals, but people just ran away from the Snake Slither, the Crocodile Walk and the Polar Bear Promenade because they didn't want to be eaten. Which is fair enough.

'Can you see her?' Dennis asked Gnasher, who pointed. Dennis caught a glimpse of a yellow-and-black jumper.

'She's right in the middle of all these penguins,' said Dennis. He was actually a bit relieved because there are a lot worse places to be lost than in the middle of a parade of penguins. Like a crowd of unhappy hippos.

'Worst parade ever!' a loud voice boomed. 'Shoulders back! Arms straight! Left, right, left, right, left . . .'

'Oh no!' said Dennis. 'It's the Colonel! If he sees Bea, he's bound to tell Mum and Dad!'

Every day the Colonel came to the zoo to tell the penguins they weren't very good at parading. Dennis snuck up beside the Colonel and got his attention.

PSST!

BEANO

'What was that?' said the Colonel, surprised. 'Are you talking to me?'

'I love the smell of pork pies in the morning,' said Dennis mysteriously.

'I don't quite follow you,' said the Colonel.

'It's a spy code,' Dennis said. 'I say what I just said then you give me the password. Then I can pass on my top-secret information.'

The Colonel gasped. He knew what was going on. This chap was one of those enemy agents he'd been tasked with keeping an eye on the other night! The blighter had mistaken him for one of his fellow agents. If the Colonel was clever, he could capture the spy, save the world and get another medal!

'I forgot the password,' said the Colonel, not very cleverly. 'Could you give me a hint?'

'Well done,' said Dennis. '"I forgot the password" is the password. Now listen very carefully, I shall say this only once. Operation Pork Pie starts tomorrow.'

'About turn! Quick march,' the Colonel cried, striding off in the direction of the police station to ruin Sergeant Slipper's day.

'Heh!' chuckled Dennis. 'That got rid of him! Now to find Bea!'

Dennis followed the penguin parade into the zoo. Every now and then he caught a glimpse of a little human arm or leg, so he knew Bea was in there somewhere.

'Dennis!' cried a voice.

'Harsha! You got away!' said Dennis, delighted to see his friend again.

'It was a sticky situation,' said Harsha, 'but I put five bubblegum balls in my mouth and blew a bubble the size of a house . . .'

'Ooh,' said Dennis. 'Did you float up, up and away?'

'No,' said Harsha. 'It burst all over the manager and I ran away while he tried to get it off.'

HA-HA! I BET YOU WEREN'T POP-ULAR!

Dennis would have asked more, but he still had a bigger problem to solve.

'Bea's in the penguin parade,' he explained. 'So we just have to wait until they get back to their enclosure and then we can rescue her and take her home.'

'Cool,' said Harsha, scanning the penguins for Bea. 'I see her jumper . . . oh blast, it's gone again!'

'Harsha,' said Dennis, stopping. 'Do you think I'm a bad person?'

'What? No!' said Harsha. 'Why?'

'I was so keen to have fun that I forgot to look after someone really important,' said Dennis. 'And look what happened. This is all my fault, Harsha.'

'Bad things happen all the time,' said Harsha. 'It doesn't have to be anyone's fault, and it's how you react that shows what kind of person you are. You're trying to fix things now, aren't you?'

'Yes,' said Dennis. 'But I feel like a terrible big brother.'

'Heena and I fight all the time,' said Harsha, 'but I know that if I need help she will be there for me, and she knows I'd be there for her. You're doing the same for Bea. You're a great big brother!'

'Thanks,' said Dennis, cheering up a bit. 'And you're a great friend.'

'Gnash-gnash!' yowled Gnasher. Bea had popped out of the penguin parade and was pulling faces at a monkey on a branch.

The monkey pulled a face back. Bea giggled, but she didn't see the monkey's long tail curling down towards her.

'Look out, Bea!' cried Dennis, but it was too late. The monkey's tail looped round his little sis and lifted her right over the wall and into Monkey Island!

NO! THAT BEASTLY BABOON'S GOT BABY BEA!

Chapter Eleven

Monkey Business

Monkey Island is where the zoo's monkeys and apes hang out. It is indeed an island, with a moat running all the way around it. The trees on the island are very big, so their branches have grown over the moat.

If you watch long enough, you sometimes see a sleeping monkey fall off a branch and into the moat. The only thing funnier than a sleeping monkey falling into water is a sleepy monkey trying to swim.

Bea loves monkeys and apes, and she was super-excited to finally be on Monkey Island. She likes how cheeky the monkeys look, but most of all she loves it when the chimps throw poo around. And today the poo was flying!

Crowds of kids were gathered, laughing and pointing at the monkeys and apes, and lots of grown-ups were tutting and pretending that they disapproved, while secretly enjoying the spectacle too. When the monkey carrying Bea finally put her down on a branch, she waved to the people watching.

Dennis gulped. Bea was sitting on a branch in a very big tree, surrounded by lots of monkeys. One mischievous-looking monkey sat beside her picking its nose, then suddenly shoved Bea off the branch!

Dennis and Harsha held their breath, waiting for the splash that would tell them she'd fallen in the moat. The splash didn't come – instead, the monkey caught Bea with

its tail. Then it swung her to and fro, higher and higher . . . and let go.

Dennis and Harsha held their breath – again – but another monkey caught tumbling Bea's ankle with his tail and tossed her to the next monkey! Soon Bea was flying from monkey to monkey, giggling and squealing with delight.

Dennis ran to the farthest end of the monkey enclosure, with Gnasher and Harsha right behind him. If the last monkey threw Bea out of Monkey Island, then he would be there to catch her.

Sure enough, when Bea had travelled along the line of monkeys, the last one gave her an extra big swing and she flew right out of Monkey Island.

'I'll catch you, Bea!' yelled Dennis, but Bea

passed way over his head, way over Harsha's head and way over Gnasher's.

OH NO!

HELLO, DEN–DEN! HELLO, HARSH–HAR!, HELLO, GNASH–GNASH!

OH GNO!

In fact, Bea flew right over the gap between Monkey Island and straight into Ellis the elephant's enclosure.

Ellis looked up and extended his trunk into the air. Bea grabbed it, twirled around it a couple of times, then slid down the trunk, along Ellis's back and down his tail.

Ooh, that tickles, thought Ellis, and a little shudder made him flick his tail. Bea again flew through the air, this time vanishing through a window, into the Reptile House!

BEANOTOWN ZOO

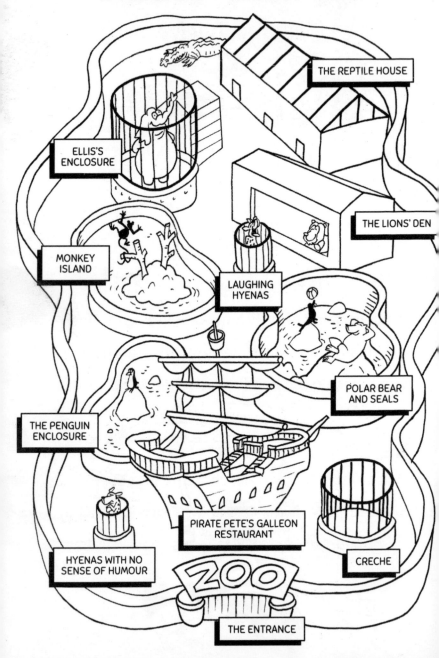

Chapter Twelve

Leapin' Lizards

'After her!' cried Dennis, charging into the

Reptile House. It was hot and sweaty inside.

Harsha put her face to the first glass window.

'There she is,' she cried.

Bea was sliding down a giant coiled python as though it was a helter-skelter. When she landed on the floor of the snake's house, the python hissed towards her, but quick-thinking Bea picked up two chameleons from the floor of the enclosure. She pointed one upwards, and the chameleon shot its sticky tongue out and attached itself to the ceiling.

Those chameleons are very chilled. They must be calmer chameleons. – The Ed

By using her chameleon chums to swing on, Bea made her way to the other end of the Reptile House, where she let go and made a perfect landing on a knobbly log floating in the middle of a pond.

'She's safe!' cried Dennis. 'I thought that snake was going to eat her!'

But then something odd happened. The log opened its eyes, then opened its enormous mouth, which was full of big teeth. It wasn't a log – it was a crocodile!

Bea leaped off the crocodile and onto the next log, then the next, and then the last one.

Those logs *also* turned out to be crocodiles, and they were pretty annoyed! The last croc flicked its tail and launched Bea into the air.

She disappeared over the wall of the Reptile House, and then . . . silence.

'Oh no,' said Harsha. 'Dennis, that's the lion enclosure!'

Dennis fainted.

Dennis woke up with a cold, wet face.

Gnasher was licking him.

'Get off, Gnasher!' said Dennis, getting up. They dashed to the window in the wall of the Lions' Den to see what had happened to poor little Bea.

She was playing with two lion cubs, giggling and pushing them around while they pretended to pounce on her. A lioness lying nearby got to her feet and walked towards Bea.

Was it going to eat her?

Dennis fainted. Again!

This time he woke up cold and wet because Harsha was licking his face.

'Well, it worked last time when Gnasher licked you,' Harsha said, while Dennis dried his face with his jumper.

They ran back to the window to see what

had happened to Bea, Dennis's insides tied up in knots.

What he saw nearly had him fainting *again* – this time with relief.

The lioness was licking her two cubs and Bea clean, like any good mum would!

Good to see Bea lion down, she must be feline okay! – The Ed

The lioness looked up, then ushered her cubs away as a little vehicle sped across the den towards them.

'It's Rubi!' shouted Dennis. And it was!

Rubi whizzed across the grass of the lion enclosure at top speed, scooped Bea up into her arms, then headed back the way she had come, pursued by a couple of male lions (who were too lazy to try *really* hard to catch her).

'Let's go,' said Harsha, heading for the gate
to the Lions' Den. A zookeeper was watching
anxiously and, when Rubi was safely out, he
flicked a big switch and the gate clanged shut.
Rubi and Bea were safe!

'Rubes . . .' said Dennis, almost lost for
words. He took Bea and gave her a huge, big-
bro cuddle. 'How?' he asked Rubi, finally.

'Well,' grinned Rubi. 'The sun charged my chair's battery pretty quickly and I thought I'd use my drone to see if there was anything I could do to help. I spotted Bea and whizzed over here. When I told the zookeeper there was a baby in the Lion's Den, he didn't need a lot of persuasion for *me* to go in there instead of *him*, the big scaredy-cat!'

'You're amazing,' said Harsha admiringly.

Dennis's phone rang.

'Oh no,' he said. 'It's Mum!'

HI, MUM. HOW'S THE WEDDING?

YES, EVERYTHING IS FINE HERE. BEA? SHE'S RIGHT HERE. I THINK SHE'S GOING TO GO FOR A NAP.

THE NOISES? NO, IT ISN'T LIONS ROARING, IT'S ... ER, JUST THE GAME I'M PLAYING. YES, SEE YOU LATER. BYE.

Dennis hung up. 'She's gone,' he said, then double-checked that he *had* actually hung up.

PHEE-EW!

It was time to go home.

Dennis picked Bea up, and the friends made their way slowly out of the zoo. As they walked past Monkey Island, Bea waved to all her furry friends, who whooped enthusiastically and threw poo at the big viewing window.

Where it hit the glass it stuck, forming a perfect portrait of their pal.

'That's poo-tiful,' said Harsha.

Chapter Thirteen

Home, Sweet Home

When Mum and Dad got home later that night, they found Dennis and Harsha asleep on the sofa. Heena was on her phone.

'Hi,' said Heena. 'How was the wedding?'

'Boring,' said Mum, taking off her shoes.

'Apart from when the bride accidentally set fire to her bouquet and the vicar emptied the font over her to put it out,' added Dad.

'Was everything OK here?' asked Mum.

'Fine,' lied Heena. 'Pretty quiet, really.' For her, at least. She'd only noticed the kids were missing when they'd returned home. On the bright side, she'd helped her friend Steph make up with her boyfriend.

Dennis and Harsha stirred.

'Hello, Harsha. Did you come over to keep Dennis and Heena company?' Mum asked. 'That was thoughtful of you.'

'Hmmm-mmm,' Harsha mumbled sleepily.

Mum and Dad went upstairs to check on Bea. She was safe and sound in her cot, and Mum was touched to see Gnasher asleep at the door, guarding the littlest Menace.

'Aw, look,' she said. 'Even Gnasher's keeping an eye on Bea.'

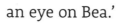

Downstairs, Dennis was grinning.

ALL'S WELL THAT ENDS WELL, THAT'S WHAT I NEVER SAY!

'I can't believe we're going to get away with what happened today,' said Heena.

Mum and Dad came back into the living room with their arms crossed.

'Er, there's just one thing, Dennis . . .'

'Yes?' said Dennis, innocently, his heart suddenly hammering in his chest.

'Why is Gnasher wearing a nappy?'

'Time for us to go!' said Heena, suddenly getting up. 'Come on, Harsha! It's late.'

'Why is Gnasher wearing a nappy?' repeated Dennis, thinking fast.

'Because . . . er . . .'

'That was me,' said Harsha. 'I'd never changed a baby's nappy, so Dennis said I could copy what he did to Bea, only on Gnasher. And he looked kind of cute wearing it, so we just left it on him.'

Mum bought the lie and ruffled Dennis's hair.

WELL, AREN'T YOU THE STAR BABYSITTER AFTER ALL?

Chapter Fourteen

The Bit After Dennis Got Away With It

WHO WANTS THE NEXT ONE?

The next morning, Dennis was up bright and early, as he always was on a Sunday (there's no school on a Sunday, so there's nothing to stay in bed for).

Dad was making his legendary pancakes, so there was sticky pancake batter everywhere, including the ceiling. Gnasher was licking some off Bea's leg.

'Paper's here,' said Mum, unfolding the Beanotown Sunday Gazette. 'It seems there was a bit of a fuss over a baby yesterday.'

Dennis choked on his pancake.

'Are you OK?' Dad asked. Dennis nodded vigorously.

'Some people just can't be trusted with children,' said Dad, flipping a pancake right

SOMEONE LET A BABY OUT ON ITS OWN, WHICH THEN CAUSED HAVOC AT THE SWEETIE SHACK, RAN RIOT AT BEANOLAND AND ALMOST GOT EATEN BY LIONS AT THE ZOO!

Beanotown Gazette

BABY BOTHER IN BEANOTOWN

over his shoulder, over the table and onto Bea's head. **'Whoops!'**

Dennis got up from the table. 'I'm . . . just, er . . . going to take Bea out for a walk.'

'Are you sure?' asked Dad. 'There are more pancakes coming.'

Dennis lifted Bea out of her high chair. 'I'm sure. Come on, Bea.'

'Oh my days!' said Mum. 'It says here the monkeys made a picture of the baby . . . with poo!' She held the paper out to Dad.

Dad laughed, then squinted at the picture
a bit. 'I know it's poo and everything, but does
that baby look familiar to you?'

Mum looked at the picture again.

'It can't be . . . can it?'

'He couldn't have . . . *could* he?'

Dennis shut the front door.

'Shall we go fast, Bea?' he asked his baby
sister. Bea loved to zoom in her pushchair!

'VROOM!' said Bea, pointing down the
path excitedly.

'Let's go!' cried Dennis. They got to the
corner of Gasworks Road and Bash Street
when they heard it. A cry, half angry, half
anguished:

Dennis stopped. 'Did you hear that?'

Bea shook her head.

Gnope, thought Gnasher.

'I didn't think so,' said Dennis with a wink, and off they sped.

Just a boy, his baby sister and his awesome dog, off on another adventure.

School Academic Diary

SINGLY-TERM HOMEWORK PLAN

Name....................
Class....................
Teacher....................

MANUAL OF MISCHIEF!

HOME ALONE
ξ SPECIAL! ς

How to Tame a Babysitter!

your house, your RULES!

Babysitters BANNED!

[TOP SECRET!]

When parents are away, it's time to PLAY...

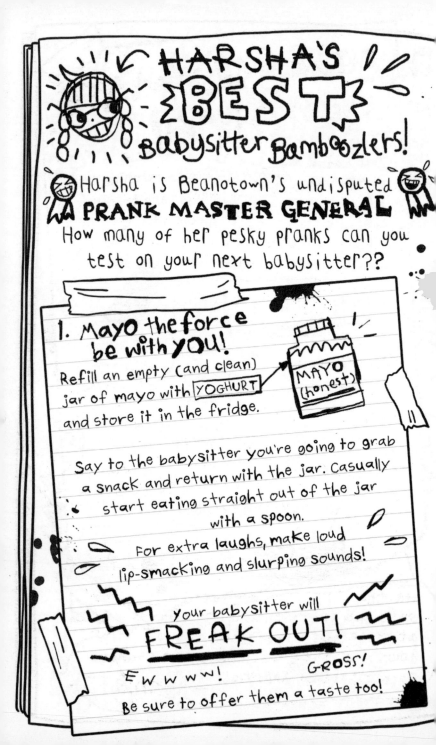

2. Take ULTIMATE CONTROL!

Babysitters love to chill-out, watching telly. So, use a tiny piece of black tape to cover up the sensor on your TV remote.

Don't forget to set the telly to your fave 'toon channel before you do this.

RESULT!!

Be sure to tell your babysitter how amazing it is that they have the same cool taste in telly as you do!

Harsha says she tests these at home before writing them down — so they each have The Chandra Family Seal of Approval! —DENNIS

3. PHONE = ALONE!

If your babysitter is guzzling too much free wi-fi, there's a simple way to stretch their patience ...

This is the perfect prank to teach someone who's <u>obsessed</u> with their phone too!

Find a time when they're away from their phone, and simply wind as many rubber bands as possible around it – until it's completely covered! Thick ones, thin ones, coloured ones – the more the merrier!!!!

Sneak the phone back where you found it and wait until the next time your babysitter goes to use it!
It's even better if someone calls them!

4. Totally Buggin' ~ Behaviour!

Plant an upside-down mug on a table where the babysitter can't miss it.

Stick a label on top that says →

WORLD'S BEST BABY-SITTER.

BEE TRAPPED INSIDE!
please take outside!

Most babysitters will ignore it,

SURPRISE!!

BUT...

Underneath the mug, place another note saying →

MUG

OMG!! you take orders from MUGS!!

LOL

5. Cookies + SCREAM!!

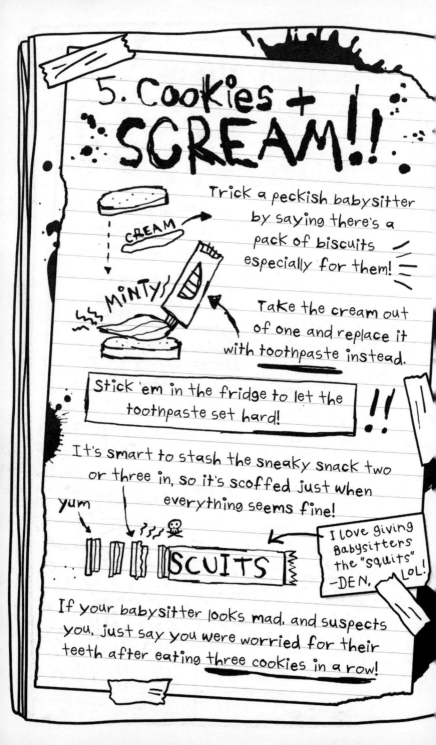

Trick a peckish babysitter by saying there's a pack of biscuits especially for them!

CREAM

MINTY

Take the cream out of one and replace it with toothpaste instead.

Stick 'em in the fridge to let the toothpaste set hard!

!!

It's smart to stash the sneaky snack two or three in, so it's scoffed just when everything seems fine!

yum

SCUITS

I love giving babysitters the "squits" -DEN, LOL!

If your babysitter looks mad, and suspects you, just say you were worried for their teeth after eating three cookies in a row!

6. BUBBLE TROUBLE!

Hide a large piece of bubble wrap under a rug where your babysitter is likely to walk. When they step on the rug, they'll make popping noises.

POP

POP

POP

That's your signal to turn and look at them with a look of shock!

Hold your nose, shake your head and watch them turn red at the pumpy-sounding pops!

What drink can you make with bubble wrap?

POP!

Ha-ha-ha!

7. WATER WALLY!

Walk up to your babysitter and give them two plastic cups, filled with water.

Tell them you want to balance the cups on your hands, but you need their help.

Hold your hands out, palms down. Ask them to balance a cup on each hand.

Skillz!

WOAH!!

Once both are balanced, say 'Awesome!' and ask your babysitter to remove them.

8. How to Make Your Babysitter
BUZZ OFF!

Sneak a raisin into a paper towel and hold it as you pretend to swat an imaginary fly, making sure that your babysitter is watching.

After a while, yell

GOTCHA!
Pesky fly!

Then bend down to pick up the 'fly' (the raisin!) using your napkin, then scoff the raisin in front of your babysitter.

They'll think that you've eaten a REAL FLY. Tell them, you think it's too much hassle to tidy up properly...and the more protein you eat, the better!

THE MENACE FAMILY CODE!

As told to me by Gran!

> ### with GREAT PRANKS comes GREAT RESPONSIBILITY!!!

* **Have FUN!**
  The idea is to make everyone **LAUGH!**
* Practice makes the perfect prankster.
* Have pranks and jokes ready for EVERY situation.
* A joke should NEVER BE MEAN - just funny!
* Prepare to be **pranked back** - be ready to laugh at yourself.
* Be ready to take credit (or own up!)
* If a prank backfires (someone doesn't find it funny) say **SORRY**.
* Bogeys and farts are ALWAYS funny!

signed: ☆ **DENNIS MENACE.**

About the Authors

Craig Graham and Mike Stirling were both born in Kirkcaldy, Fife, in the same vintage year when Dennis first became the cover star of Beano. Ever since, they've been training to become the Brains Behind Beano Books (which is mostly making cool stuff for kids from words and funny pictures). They've both been Beano Editors, but now Craig is Managing Editor and Mike is Editorial Director (ooh, fancy!) at Beano Studios. In the evenings they work for I.P. Daley at her Boomix factory, where Craig fetches coffee and doughnuts, and Mike hoses down her personal bathroom once an hour (at least). It's the ultimate Beano mission!

Craig lives in Fife with his wife Laura and amazing kids Daisy and Jude. He studied English so this book is smarter than it looks (just like him). Craig is partially sighted, so he bumps into things quite a lot. He couldn't be happier, although fewer bruises would be a bonus.

Mike is an International Ambassador for Dundee (where Beano started!) and he lives in Carnoustie, famous for its legendary golf course. Mike has only ever played crazy golf. At home, Mike and his wife Sam relax by untangling the hair of their adorable kids, Jessie and Elliott.